For Helen and her mad dogs

American edition published in 2010 by Andersen Press USA, an imprint of Andersen Press Ltd.
www.andersenpressusa.com

First published in Great Britain in 2007 by Andersen Press Ltd, 20 Vauxhall Bridge Road, London SW1V 2SA. Published in Australia by Random House Australia Pty., 20 Alfred Street, Milsons Point, Sydney, NSW 2061.

Distributed in the United States and Canada by
Lerner Publishing Group, Inc.
241 First Avenue North
Minneapolis, MN 55401 U.S.A.
www.lernerbooks.com

Library of Congress Cataloging-in-Publication Data Available.

ISBN: 978-0-7613-6443-6

Color separated in Switzerland by Photolitho AG, Zürich.
Printed and bound by TWP, Singapore.
This book has been printed on acid-free paper.
1 – TWP – 3/9/10

A Little Princess Story

I Want My Light On!

Tony Ross

Andersen Press USA

The Little Princess loved a story at bedtime.

But she didn't like the dark.
"I WANT MY LIGHT ON!" she said.
"Why?" asked her dad.

"Because there are ghosts in the dark," she said.
"Probably under the bed."

“Don’t be silly, there are NO such things as ghosts,”
said Dad. “And there’s nothing under the bed.”

“Don’t be silly, there are NO such things as ghosts,” said the Admiral. “And if there were, the General would deal with them.”

“Don’t be silly, there are NO such things as ghosts,” said the Doctor. “And if there were, all you’d have to do is blow your nose.”

“I WANT MY LIGHT ON ANYWAY!”
said the Little Princess.

"Why?" said the Maid.
"Look, Gilbert isn't afraid of the dark."

“I’m not so much afraid of the DARK!” said the Little Princess.
“I’m sort of more afraid of ghosts.”

“Don’t be silly, there are NO such things as ghosts,” said the Maid. “And if there were, they’d be very small, because I’VE never seen one!”

“Yes, Gilbert, ghosts are probably very small,”
said the Little Princess.

"So we must be careful not to step on them!"

“Nighty nighty, sleepy tighty,” said the Maid . . .
and she switched off the light.

“I bet ghosts are afraid of the dark as well,”
thought the Little Princess.

“OOOO!” cried the Little Princess.
“That sounds very much like a ghost!”

“OOOO!” cried the little ghost.
“That sounds very much like a little girl!”

So the Little Princess hid under her bed.

So did the little ghost.

"BOOOOOO!" said the Little Princess.

"OOOOOO!" said the little ghost.

And he ran all the way back to where he lived
at the top of the castle.

"MOM, MOM, I'VE SEEN A LITTLE GIRL!"

"Don't be silly," said his mom.
"There are NO such things as little girls!"
"I WANT MY LIGHT ON ANYWAY!"
said the little ghost. "Just in case."

Other Little Princess Picture Books

I Want TWO Birthdays!